T0145043

AuthorHouse™
1663 Liberty Drive
Bloomington, IN 47403
www.authorhouse.com
Phone: 833-262-8899

Because of the dynamic nature of the Internet, any web addresses or links contained in this book may have changed since publication and may no longer be valid. The views expressed in this work are solely those of the author and do not necessarily reflect the views of the publisher, and the publisher hereby disclaims any responsibility for them.

This book is printed on acid-free paper.

ISBN: 978-1-6655-0648-9 (sc)
ISBN: 978-1-6655-0650-2 (hc)
ISBN: 978-1-6655-0649-6 (e)

Print information available on the last page.

Published by AuthorHouse 10/31/2020

authorHOUSE®

About the Author:

Myra is a counselor, author, and entrepreneur. Myra Sampson Reeves is a native of Philadelphia, PA. She is a graduate of Wesley Theological Seminary in Washington, D.C. where she earned her MA degree with a focus on pastoral counseling and missions. Myra currently resides in Washington, D.C. where she works as an early childhood specialist at Centro Nia. Myra is a mother of three wonderful sons, Zuogwi, Mlynue Alfred, and Yuejay Thomas Henry Reeves. Her passions are writing, reading, painting and Missionary work. Myra's dream is to become an entrepreneur and curator of a museum. She is the author of "Liberian Culture and Marriages," 2007, self published at Drexel University Printing Company.

About the Illustrator:

Emily grew up in Upstate N.Y. and moved to Northern Virginia in 2014. Emily is an artist and illustrator, having worked on various personal and freelance projects. She has a BA degree in Studio Art (2008) and a certificate in Character Animation (2011). Emily primarily works in oil paints, but also enjoys working in gouache, watercolor, acrylic paints, and inks. Her favorite subjects are animals, pet portraits, and flowers. Emily is also a manager at her family's shop, Manassas Olive Oil Company, in Old Town Manassas, VA, and also teaches evening art classes at the Center for the Arts. When she isn't working or creating, she enjoys going for walks with her dog, Sully. She also enjoys the company of her cats, rabbits, and chickens.

Follow her on instagram at: EmilyThomson_Art

Dedication Page:

This book is dedicated to my beloved family Father, Alfred O. Sampson, and Mother Emma Sampson, who inspired me to follow my dreams. To my beloved siblings, Joanna, thank you for your moral support of encouragement and resiliency to pursue my dreams.

To my beloved brother who encouraged me to soar like an eagle, to be kind and honest towards others, and to remember our family heritage. Thank you both!

The Dream Catcher symbolizes the dream of the Native Cherrokee who dreams of prosperity, happiness, and love. While the negative dreams are disbursed into a web, the positive dreams remain embedded into the web that allows the following positivity to enter into one's life.

It is Sunday Afternoon, and we are preparing to spend the day at Atlantic city, New Jersey on the boardwalk and beach. As dad gets the car ready, I call all of my friends, Sharon, Robin, Sandy and Rhonda inviting them to the beach for the day. We gather our bags and towels and off we go!

Fun, Fun, Fun, its time for the morning cycling on the boardwalk! While we were riding our bikes we met a man named Mr. Thomas walking his dog, named Captain. We began riding our bikes faster as we hear Rhonda say,

"Good Bye Captain!"

Now we are walking to the Steel Pier for the amusement rides and games. At the game stands we see the winning prizes; stuffed bears, tigers, elephants and giraffes. Wow we were in amazement! Sandy, Robin, and Sharon said, "Get on the swings!" While Myra and Rhonda said, "Lets get on the Merry-Go-Round!"

Sharon yells, "LET'S ALL GET ON THE SWINGS!"

Robin, Rhonda, Sandy, Myra and Sharon board the swings. The swings start slow and then goes higher and higher, and it feels like we are flying! Round, round we go, higher and higher. We all yell out, feeling overwhelmed with joy and laughter, shouting, "FASTER, FUN FUN, LET'S DO IT AGAIN!"

Sandy points over to the Merry-Go-Round, Myra replies, "Let's all get on your favorite color horse and ride it!"

Off we go round, and round, up and down on the carousel saying, "Getty up, getty up!!!"

Rhonda says, "It's time for us to go to the beach! YAY!!!!! Let's Go!"

Lets go!!!

Robin, Sharon, Sandy, Rhonda and Myra dash into the water. Sandy starts swimming out into the waves while Robin says, "Look at the beautiful seagulls flying above!"

While Myra notices the two red and white sailboats from afar.

Rhonda and Sharon continue jumping the waves.

"It's time for Sand Play!," says Myra.

Sandy says, "Let's build some sand castles!"

Robin began digging, "I will build the pool!"

While Rhonda and Robin decided to collect sea shells and sea weed in their pail buckets.

"ICE CREAM! Ice Cream, who wants Ice Cream? Come and get your Ice Cream! I have water ice, ice cream sandwiches and much more!" Shouted the Ice cream man.

We all decided to get our favorite Popsicles- cherry, lemon, blueberry, Strawberry and Orange!

"Look! Look up! There's the blimp, it says, 'Welcome to Atlantic City!' And, look over there, there are the life guards with their safety boats!

"That's so cool!" replied Myra and Sandy.

"I'm hungry," said Robin. Dad calls out, "Let's go girls and get something to eat!"

"I will have pizza," said Robin.

"I want hotdogs and fries," replied Sandy and Sharon.

Myra and Rhonda decided to have hamburgers and fries.

"Look, there's the museum! Let's go visit the Ripley's Believe It or not Museum!"

I would like to see the beautiful waterfalls, Wax people, Monsters and inventions by the scientists and then ride on the time machine!

Peanuts, peanuts everywhere! Some like them hot, some like them with salt. Some come with shells, most come without. GET YOU FRESH HOT ROASTED PEANUTS HERE! Buy one and get one free!

Come one, come all to Irene's Souvenir shop! We sell postcards, toys, candy, souvenir gifts and t-shirts for all! Sandy said, "I would like to buy a teddy bear!

"Oh," said Robin and Sharon, "I would like to buy a beach ball!" While Myra said she wanted to buy a toy train set and Rhonda decided to buy a bracelet.

Dad calls out, "Girls, this is our last stop to the Ice Cream Parlor!"

Some of the girls order vanilla ice cream cones while others order vanilla chocolate swirl and water ice.

"Now is the time to visit the Salt Water Taffy shop to pick up some gifts for your parents," said Mr. Sampson. Sandy, Myra, Sharon, Robin and Rhonda delightfully ran into the Salt Water Taffy store. Some chose chocolate fudge while others chose the traditional assortments of lemon, cherry, lime, and rainbow flavored taffy.

"It's time for us to say goodbye to Atlantic City girls," said Mr Sampson. "I hope you girls enjoyed your visit and one day soon before the summer ends, we will return."

The girls waved bye bye, as the car headed home.

Special thanks to my childhood church, Richardson Memorial Presbyterian Church. My beloved families of 6157 Sansom Street. A note of appreciation to my beloved friends Linda, Leslie and Wendy.

My spiritual mentors Minister Thema Pugh and Ms. Kathy Brown. A world of thanks to my church family at Shiloh Baptist Church. To my artistic, proficient and talented illustrator, thank you for your dedication.

Printed in the United States
By Bookmasters